Viz Graphic Novel

FLAME OF RECCA™

Vol. 8

Story & Art by Nobuyuki Anzai

D1351150

Contents

Flame of Recca
Vol. 8
Gollancz Manga Edition

Story and Art by
Nobuyuki Anzai

English Adaptation/Lance Caselman
Translation/Joe Yamazaki
Touch-Up & Lettering/Kelle Han
Graphics & Cover Design/Sean Lee
Editors/Eric Searleman
UK Cover Adaptation/Sue Michniewicz

1 3 5 7 9 10 8 6 4 2

The right of Nobuyuki Anzai to be identified as the author of this work has been asserted by him in accordance with the Copyright, Designs and Patents Act 1988.

A CIP catalogue record for this book is available from the British Library

ISBN-13 978 0 57508 086 7

Printed and bound by GGP, Germany

www.orionbooks.co.uk

Part Sixty-Eight:
The One Kurei Protects

605

GENERAL AIR!!

ROYAL WAVE!

4

K·O
WIN
OOOH!

ACTION!!!

TOO BAD, RECCA...

AW...

BZZZZ

BAD GRAPHICS

ME, TOO!!

FULL HOUSE!

THEY CAN NEVER SIT STILL. HERE YA GO, TWO PAIR!

WHY DO IDIOTS HAVE SO MUCH ENERGY?

OKAY.

ONE MORE, SAICHO!! THIS TIME I'LL USE--

YOW!!

FINGER SLAP! ♥

SHWAK

SHWAK

A LITTLE RELAX-ATION ...

NO ONE CAN REMAIN ON GUARD AT ALL TIMES.

GIVE THEM A BREAK, TOKIYA.

IS NECES-SARY.

HEH.

LOOK AT THE FOOLS.

WE HAVE FAR TO GO TO REACH OUR OBJECTIVE. A BREAK IS GOOD.

ARE YOU LISTENING?

UH-HUNH ...

YOU SEE, I...

CONSTANTLY THINKING ABOUT WINNING AND LOSING, LIVING AND DYING, CAN WEAR ONE DOWN.

YOU MEAN KUREI.

OBJECTIVE ...

DON'T YOU THINK IT'S STRANGE?

THAT THERE'S ONE PERSON EVEN KUREI WON'T DEFY?

KAGERŌ...

YES. BUT YOU HAVE A DIFFERENT OBJECTIVE...

WHO IS HE?

THE HOST OF THE TOURNAMENT? MORI KŌRAN!!

KŌRAN IS A KING OF THE UNDERWORLD. KUREI CALLS HIM FATHER, THOUGH KŌRAN'S BLOOD DOES NOT FLOW IN HIS VEINS.

BUT KUREI, WHO COULD KILL KŌRAN AT ANY TIME, HUMBLY OBEYS HIM.

I DON'T KNOW WHAT TIE BINDS THEM.

...

I DON'T KNOW.

BUT...

IT IS A MYSTERY.

WUPWUPWUP WUPWUPWUP

1:13 A.M., IN THE MOUNTAINS OF "I" PREFECTURE--

WARWARWARWAR

MR. KUREI.

GOOD TO SEE YOU AGAIN...

WOOOO

YOUR MOTHER IS WAITING.

MOTHER
...

WHERE...

...AM I?

I ARRIVED IN THIS ERA....

DRIFTING THROUGH TIME AND SPACE ...

KUREI !?!

A KIND WORD AND A KIND HAND.

I MET THE WOMAN WHO BECAME MY MOTHER.

LITTLE BOY?

ARE YOU LOST ...

IT'S BEEN SO LONG.

IT'S SO GOOD TO SEE YOU. COME CLOSER.

LET ME SEE YOUR FACE.

SHK

HOLD YOUR TONGUES, MAGGOTS!

OR I'LL GUT YOU!!

HE MISSES HIS MOMMY.

THE LITTLE PANSY.

HE MIGHT BE THE HEAD OF URUHA, BUT HE'S JUST A KID.

HMPH.

WE'VE BEEN ORDERED TO GUARD MRS. KŌRAN'S PALACE.

WE DON'T WORK FOR KUREI, WE'RE MR. KŌRAN'S BODYGUARDS!

BUT IF YOU KILL US, YOU'LL BE IN BIG TROUBLE.

WHOA! JUST KIDDING, MR. RAIHA!

STAND DOWN, RAIHA! OUT OF RESPECT FOR MOTHER.

YOU--

BUT REMEMBER, MR. KUREI!

HEH, SURE.

NOW LEAVE US ALONE.

NO FUNNY STUFF, OR MAMA GETS IT!

KLAK

14

HERE'S STILL LOVE N YOU! HEH HEH HEH!

DO YOU LOVE TSUKINO? SHE'S LIKE A MOTHER TO YOU, EH?

KUREI!!

YOU TWO MAKE AN INTERESTING COUPLE...

A CHILD WITHOUT A MOTHER.

A MOTHER WITHOUT A CHILD.

THERE WAS A REASON WHY I ALLOWED TSUKINO TO CODDLE YOU AND RAISED YOU UNTIL NOW!

STOP!!

LET ME BE WITH HER!!

LET GO OF HER!!

STRUGGLE!

SUFFER!!

CURSE ME!!!

ID YOURSELF OF USELESS EMOTIONS!!

DO YOU WANT LOVE, KUREI?

LOVE IS DEBILITATING RUBBISH!!

YOU ARE A MACHINE!

IS AN UNBREAK-ABLE LEASH!!!

THE BOND BETWEEN MOTHER AND CHILD...

YOUR LOVE FOR TSUKINO ENSURES YOUR LOYALTY!!

BUT NOW IT'S TIME FOR YOU TO BECOME THE AGENT OF MY DREAMS!!

SON
...

KUREI!

DON'T WORRY ABOUT ME. YOUR VISITS ARE ALL I NEED.

NOW GO! WE MUSTN'T PROVOKE KŌRAN.

I'M SORRY I WASN'T ABLE TO BE THERE FOR YOU.

I LIVE FOR THE DAY WHEN WE CAN BE TOGETHER AGAIN.

COME BACK TO ME SAFE.

KUREI...

I'LL BE BACK.

HSSK

YOU'D BETTER NOT COME HERE TOO OFTEN.

ABOUT TIME YOU LEFT.

OKAY...

WE'RE GOING, RAIHA.

UNLESS YOU WANT MAMA TO BECOME DOG MEAT.

MASTER MŌRAN COULD DECIDE TO PUSH THE BUTTON.

THERE'S A TINY REMOTE-CONTROL BOMB IMPLANTED IN MRS. MŌRAN!!

BUT MY FATHER HASN'T TAUGHT YOU LOWLIFES PROPER ETIQUETTE.

I RESTRAINED MYSELF EARLIER FOR MY MOTHER'S SAKE...

TO SPARE HER THE SIGHT OF BLOOD-SHED.

WMP

YOU...

WE'RE MASTER MORAN'S---

WHOA, WAIT!!

THAT I FIRED THEM!

I'LL LET FATHER KNOW...

FOOSH

N-NO PROBLEM.

SHAKE...

YES, SIR...

I'LL BE YOUR DOG AWHILE LONGER.

I'LL PLAY ALONG FOR NOW.

YOU'RE TAINTED BY GREED. YOU MADE YOUR OWN WIFE A HOSTAGE.

BUT YOU'LL LEARN THAT YOUR METHODS ARE A SWORD THAT CUTS BOTH WAYS!!

Part Sixty-Nine:
Live (1) The Night Before

I WAS INSIDE THAT WEIRD CASTLE NEAR THE MURDER DOME.

HOMURA

I HEARD STRANGE THINGS ...

WHILE I WAS THERE ...

WELL, IF YOU HAVE A TASTE FOR LONG SHOTS, BET ON HOKAGE. THE ODDS AGAINST THEM ARE HUGE.

I'M AFRAID NOT. I LOST A FORTUNE ON KU.

WINNING, SO FAR?

THE MASKED MEN WERE DISCUSSING THE FIGHTS LIKE THEY WERE HORSE RACES.

LONG SHOTS ... ODDS ...

LOSSES ...

WINS ...

FW OOM

THERE'S A LOT BEHIND THE SCENES HERE WE DON'T KNOW ABOUT!

WE'D BETTER BE CAREFUL.

KREESH

SMSMSH

FEELS GOOD, HOMURA!!

FWURP FWURP

YEAH!

O MY LOVELY PRINCESS! YOUR FAITHFUL SHINOBI WILL LOOK AFTER YOU, NO MATTER WHAT.

I'LL PROTECT YOU!!

SLIGHTLY MISTAKEN

NO MATTER WHAT THE SCHEME IS!!

VREE

HA! I'M BURSTING WITH ENERGY!!

AND AFTER ONLY TWO HOURS OF SLEEP!!!

TPTPTPTP

HUH!?!

I'LL RUN A LITTLE!

THERE'S STILL TIME BEFORE DAWN!

THEY WERE ASLEEP A MINUTE AGO. WHAT ARE THEY DOING OUT HERE WALKING UNDER THE STARS?

TOKIYA AND PRINCESS!?!

SHOULD I GO? NO, THAT WOULD MAKE ME LOOK LIKE A JEALOUS WIMP!

I-I'LL JUST WATCH THEM FOR A MINUTE...

JEALOUS ANYWAY.

BA-BUMP

BA-BUMP

SHA OO

I WONDER WHERE HE WENT.

ARE YOU WORRIED?

NO ...

RECCA ISN'T HERE ...

SORRY TO DRAG YOU OUT HERE, TOKIYA.

THAT'S OKAY ...

KIND OF LIKE HER RIGHT NOW? I'D BETTER NOT POINT THAT OUT.

RECCA JUST DOES WHATEVER HE WANTS, WHENEVER HE WANTS. YOU NEVER KNOW WHEN HE'LL DECIDE TO DISAPPEAR.

HMPH

MIFUYU...

WHERE COULD RECCA BE?

YANAGI
...

WHAT
DO YOU
FEEL
FOR
RECCA?

WHAT
?

WHAT
ARE
THEY
TALKING
ABOUT?

GULP

SO I NEVER THOUGHT ABOUT IT.

I'VE NEVER REALLY SPENT TIME WITH A BOY BEFORE.

WELL...

I DON'T REALLY KNOW WHAT I FEEL.

UM, WOW... YOU CAUGHT ME OFF GUARD.

I *LIKE* HIM, BUT...

I FEEL THINGS I'VE NEVER FELT BEFORE.

WHEN I'M WITH RECCA, OR TALKING TO HIM ON THE PHONE...

DOESN'T SHE SEE?

IF THAT'S "LIKE," THE TITANIC WAS A CANOE.

I WONDER WHY?

SHE'S SO INNOCENT.

↑ DISAPPOINTED

AND I FEEL WEIRD WHEN I SEE HIM WITH ANOTHER GIRL...

LIKE MY HEART IS BEING SQUEEZED...

AND I FEEL LONELY WHEN I'M NOT WITH HIM...

HMM

I SHOULDN'T HAVE ASKED.

SORRY.

WHAT'S WRONG?

OKAY.

OW!!

OH, I'M SUCH A KLUTZ...

I CAN'T HEAL MYSELF...

SOMEDAY YOU'LL KNOW WHAT THOSE FEELINGS MEAN.

DON'T WORRY ABOUT IT NOW.

HUH?

WHOA, WHOA ...HEY!

OH ...

BA DUM

I'LL PROTECT HER ANYWAY.

I WON'T LET WHAT HAPPENED TO MY SISTER HAPPEN TO HER.

I DON'T CARE IF SHE DOES LOVE RECCA.

THE RAILING IS RUSTY. THAT SHOULD PREVENT TETANUS.

33

PROTECT YOUR PRINCESS FROM KUREI, NOT ME.

YOU'RE NOT THE ONLY ONE WHO CARES ABOUT YANAGI.

OW...

FM UMP

I'LL PROTECT HER FROM ANY THREAT!!

SLAM

STOP IT, YOU TWO!!

STOP!!

KNOW THIS, TOKIYA...

URUHA-OTO!!

IN DAY THREE'S FIRST FIGHT, WE HAVE AN ALL-WOMAN TEAM!!!

LED BY THE CHARMING AND HANDSOME RECCA! ♡

FACING THEM IS HOKAGE!!!

HEY, THE REF'S GOT A FAVORITE.

WOW!! THEY'RE HOT!!!

I'VE FOUND MY TEAM!!

GET 'EM, GIRLS! ♡

??

THEY'RE ACTING WEIRD.

WHAT'S WITH RECCA AND TOKIYA?

↑ KAORU

37

DISCORD PRIES AT THE USUALLY UNIFIED HOKAGE.

DAY THREE OF THE URABUTO-SATSUJIN-- ONLY 16 TEAMS REMAIN.

TOKIYA, A RIFT HAS OPENED.

BETWEEN RECCA AND ...

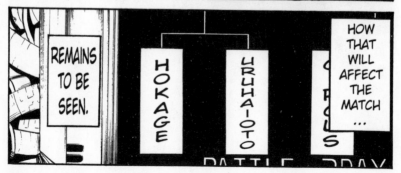

REMAINS TO BE SEEN.

HOW THAT WILL AFFECT THE MATCH ...

HOKAGE

URUHAIOTO

39

Part Seventy:
Live (2) The Curtain Rises

HOKAGE IS A MIXED-SEX TEAM OF FIVE!!

THE NUMERICAL ADVANTAGE MAY SEEM TO FAVOR HOKAGE, BUT...

THOUGH SMALL, HE'S A HIGHLY SKILLED FIGHTER! HE WILL BE SORELY MISSED BY HOKAGE!!

SORRY!

KAORU KOGANEI, WHO JOINED THE TEAM DURING THE URUHA-MABOROSHI MATCH, WILL NOT FIGHT TODAY!!

BUT...

PLEASE!

SORRY!! I'M IN BAD SHAPE TODAY! FORGIVE ME!

HUH?! WHY DIDN'T YOU TELL ME?!

TWEEK

WORD IS, SHE'S ONE OF THE BEST FEMALE FIGHTERS IN ALL THE URUHA TEAMS!

BE CAREFUL. I DON'T KNOW ABOUT THE OTHER TWO, BUT NEON IS A REAL BAD-ASS.

HE'S STILL RECOVERING FROM HIS FIGHT WITH MOKUREN.

I GAVE KAORU THE DAY OFF.

BE QUIET, RECCA.

DON'T REFUSE TO FIGHT AND THEN SCARE ME!

I'D BE GLAD TO DEAL WITH YOU BEFORE I FIGHT THEM!!!

I'LL SEW YOUR LIPS SHUT!!

DON'T YOU THINK WE CAN WIN WITHOUT HIM?

WHAT!?!

AXEKICK!

STOP IT, YOU MORONS.

Fssss

HEHHEHHEH

HANDS OFF!

YEAH, FOLLOW OUR EXAMPLE.

PLURT

KISS AND MAKE UP! NOW!!

WHAT'S WRONG WITH YOU TWO!!

WHAT'S HAPPENING TO US?

WIP

44

THEIR TIMING REALLY BLOWS.

YEAH...

NO, THIS IS DIFFERENT.

AREN'T THEY ALWAYS?

LOOK AT HOKAGE! THEY'RE ARGUING.

WUSP

WUSP

...

WATCH ME, SISTER... HA HA HA...

ONE THE OPPOSITE OF THE OTHER. NOW THAT THEY ARE DIVIDED, THEY WILL CONTINUE TO RESIST EACH OTHER.

RECCA, TOKIYA... WHAT WILL COME OF THIS?

FIRE AND WATER...

BLOC A SEMI-FINALS ROSTER

HOKAGE

URUHA-OTO

DOMON

AKI

TOKIYA

MIKI

RECCA

NEON

FUKO

SITTING OUT: KAORU
KOGANEI OF HOKAGE.
RULES: DUE TO DIFFERING
NUMBER OF FIGHTERS, A
TOURNAMENT FORMAT
WILL BE USED.

NOOOOO!!!

YEAH!!!

FIRST UP FOR HOKAGE--DOMON!!!

FIRST UP FOR URUHA-OTO--AKI!!!

SHUT UP!!!

DIE, YOU FREAK!!!

BOO

DON'T PICK ON GIRLS, YOU GORILLA!!

BOO

BOO

AKI.

YES, NEON?

REMEMBER ...

DON'T LET HIM TOUCH YOU. I DON'T WANT TO SEE ONE MARK ON YOUR BEAUTIFUL BODY.

ALL RIGHT ...

YOU'RE GIVING ME THE CREEPS !!

HEY!! WHY ARE YOU GIRLS FLIRTING WITH EACH OTHER?!

SWP!

MY SWEET ...

48

49

!!!

WAAAAAAH!!!!

HUH
?!

HUH?

?

WHY'S DOMON DANCING?

...

HEH

EEEEK!!

WAH!

HYAAH!

SNFF SWFF

HUH?

THEY'RE ... GONE?

YUCK ...

OH! OW! OW!!

SKSSSH

THERE WERE SNAKES ALL OVER ME!!

I'M NOT PLAYING AROUND!!

STOP PLAYING AROUND, FRANKEN-DICK!!

OPEN YOUR EYES AND SEE.

LET ME SHOW YOU WHAT BEAUTY IS, YOU UGLY BEAST.

KLIK...

SNAKES ?

HAS HE...

GONE NUTS?

54

SHE'S THE PERFECT OPPONENT FOR GORILLA BOY.

AKI OF THE KOTO DAMA ...

THE EFFECT OF THE KOTO DAMA STAYS WITHIN THE RING. TO THE ONLOOKERS, DOMON SEEMS TO BE INSANE.

FWOOM

SNAP OUT OF IT !!!

DOMON !!!

Part-Seventy-One:
Live (3)
Domon Finds His Groove

LIKE THIS
...

HOW'S IT WORK, MOM?! IF IT'S AN ILLUSION, HOW COME HE FEELS THE COLD ?!

SHAKE SHAKE SHAKE

F-F-FREEZ-ING...

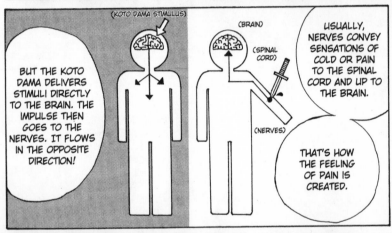

(KOTO DAMA STIMULUS)

(BRAIN)

(SPINAL CORD)

(NERVES)

BUT THE KOTO DAMA DELIVERS STIMULI DIRECTLY TO THE BRAIN. THE IMPULSE THEN GOES TO THE NERVES. IT FLOWS IN THE OPPOSITE DIRECTION!

USUALLY, NERVES CONVEY SENSATIONS OF COLD OR PAIN TO THE SPINAL CORD AND UP TO THE BRAIN.

THAT'S HOW THE FEELING OF PAIN IS CREATED.

DANGER-OUS MADOGU!

THAT'S ONE ...

AND THE THOUGHTS MAKE THE BODY FEEL THE COLD.

THE BRAIN SAYS, "IT MUST BE COLD."

ONE SEES SNOW ...

KROOSS

KRETAKET

"OPEN YOUR EYES" ACTIVATES THAT THING, RIGHT?

SO I FIGURED MY WORDS MIGHT WORK IT, TOO!!

WHAT?! HOW DID YOU CREATE AN ILLUSION?!

YOU'RE A MENTAL PYGMY!?! HOW'D YOU DO IT!?!

KRAK

70

HOW CAN THIS BE AN ILLUSION?

I'M DYING!

I'M REALLY BURNING...

MY HANDS ARE BURNING...

I CAN'T TAKE THE PAIN...

I SMELL SHEARING FLESH...

HUH?

AHEM...

WAKE UP, DOMON!!

SHINK

YOU'D PROBABLY DIE OF SHOCK...

BUT I'LL FINISH YOU OFF, ANYWAY.

IF YOU DO, I'LL GIVE YOU A KISS! ♡

WAKE UP, DOMON! ♪

WHOOSH

HAVE YOUR PHONY FLAMES BACK, KITTY CAT!!

MY DESIRE SQUELCHED IT!!

DOMON ISHIJIMA

...

SNIP

AH HA HA HA! YOU FOOL! I TOLD YOU!!

ILLUSIONS DON'T WORK ON ME!!

CHUNK

SNIP

THOUGH IT WAS FOR LUSTFUL REASONS, HIS MENTAL STRENGTH IS EXPLOSIVE!

HIS MIND IS SURPRISINGLY POWERFUL!

UNH ...

BEAK KING?

PERHAPS...

HE HAS THE POTENTIAL TO TRANSFORM DRASTICALLY!

HE HAS A STRONG MIND AS WELL.

HE IS NOT MERELY A BRUTISH OAF...

S- SISTER NEON ...

I FELL... FOR HIS TRICK...

Part Seventy-Two:
Live (4) Duo

BWA HA HA HA...

HEH HEH...

HEH

ZOOM

SLUK...

SHU!

OKAY, FUKO!!

KISS ME. ♥

YOU PROMISED!! YOU PROMISED!!

WHAT?

WHAT?

HUH?

WOOoo OOO

OH... THAT?

THEN *YOU* KISS HIM!!

WHAT?

SKRIK SKRIK

IT'S JUST A KISS.

BUT I BELIEVED YOU!!

YOU WEREN'T SERIOUS?!

DOMON, THAT WAS JUST--

TMP TMP

TMP TMP

HMM ...

OKAY ...

NOW CLOSE YOUR EYES.

NOSE HAIR

TMPTMPTMP

80

KAORU!

SORRY...

YANAGI

DON'T SAY A WORD, KAORU.

YOU'LL BE BLESSED LATER.

YEE... YECK... SHE... SHE...

REALLY? GLAD YOU LIKED IT.

YAHOO!

FUKO! YOU KISS SO SWEETLY!!

WOOSH

FNUMP

N-NEON...

UNH...

SHUOO

HUFF

HUFF

LET'S CRUSH HOKAGE.

RECCA HANABI-SHI!

!

WHAT DOES THIS MEAN?!

THE TWO REMAINING URUHA-OTO FIGHTERS HAVE BOTH ENTERED THE RING!!

I CHALLENGE YOU TO A TWO-ON-TWO DOUBLE BOUT!

I PROPOSE WE FINISH THIS MATCH NOW. WHAT DO YOU SAY?

LET'S FINISH THIS, WE TWO AGAINST YOU TWO. ♡

O - X

ONE AT A TIME TAKES TOO LONG.

DOUBLE BED?

HUH?

RECCA AND...

TOKIYA.

NO!! THAT WOMAN KNOWS THEY'RE AT ODDS!!

RECCA, TOKIYA, DON'T DO IT!!

WHAT?

I DON'T LIKE IT EITHER.

WAHOO

YEAH, NO WAY! I'D RATHER FIGHT BESIDE FUKO THAN HIM!

WHAT A BUNCH OF PUSSIES!!

HA HA HA HA HA HA !!

HA!

HEAR THAT MIKI?

HOKAGE'S SUPPOSED TO BE THE BEST. MAYBE THAT WAS BULLSHIT.

WHAT ARE YOU, FEMINISTS?

AFRAID OF YOU TWO? THAT IS FUNNY.

W/P.

SISSIES...

FORGET THEM. THEY'VE GOT NO HEART.

YEAH.

STOP, NEON. YOU'LL MAKE THEM CRY.

OKAY, THAT DOES IT!!

T O M P

SNAP

YOU DON'T SCARE ME.

CHICKEN BOY!

OR I'LL FRY YOU, BITCH!!

TAKE THAT BACK ...

THAT'S IT.

LET'S DO THIS DOUBLE BOUT!!

WE'LL USE A TWO-ON-TWO DOUBLE BOUT FORMAT!!

BOTH TEAMS ARE AGREED !!!

FOR HOKAGE--RECCA AND TOKIYA !!

FOR URUHA--OTO---NEON AND MIKI!

OKAY, RECCA.

DURING THE FIGHT, JUST STAY OUT OF MY WAY.

KISS MY ASS!

I DON'T TAKE ORDERS FROM YOU!!

IT'S FOOLISH!

THEY'RE RUSHING INTO A TRAP.

SAICHO...

THEY CAN'T FIGHT AT FULL CAPACITY.

IF THEY KEEP ON LIKE THIS...

BUT AS LONG AS THEY KEEP FIGHTING EACH OTHER..

THEY'LL BE SEVERELY WEAKENED!!

HOKAGE BEAT URUHA-MABOROSHI. I WON'T UNDERESTIMATE THEM..

I WAS RIGHT. THEY'RE NOT TO BE TAKEN LIGHTLY!

HE DODGED IT... NOT BAD.

BUT NOW, IT'S TIME TO DESTROY THEM.

YOU BUMPED INTO *ME!*

STOP SCREWING AROUND!!

FUKYOWAON-- MANIACAL HARMONY!!

HER MADOGU IS...

YOW!

PART SEVENTY·THREE: LIVE (5) HARD LOCK

URABUTOSATSUJIN,
DAY THREE

12:01 P.M.

	BLOC A		BLOC B		BLOC C		BLOC D
B O U T 1	HOKAGE VS. URUHA-OTO (CURRENTLY FIGHTING)	B O U T 1	URUHA-MA VS. URUHA-KUROGANE (CURRENTLY FIGHTING)	B O U T 1	ELEKIBRAN VS. AMONKYO (CURRENTLY FIGHTING)	B O U T 1	URUHA-KURENAI VS. KYUKI (URUHA-KURENAI WINS)
B O U T 2	CIRCUS VS. SHINSENGUMI	B O U T 2	KAIENTAI VS. HOTEI	B O U T 2	ONRYO VS. URUHA-RAI	B O U T 2	P.O.G. VS. JINMIRAIZAI (CURRENTLY FIGHTING)

EVEN A MAN AS WICKED AND POWERFUL AS GENJURO KNEW HE WAS NO MATCH FOR NEON.

SHE TURNED HIM INTO SAUSAGE MEAT...

REMEMBER YESTERDAY, SAICHO?

YES.

IF HOKAGE CAN'T DISARM...

SHE MAY EVEN BE A MATCH FOR RECCA'S FIRE DRAGONS.

SHE'S LETHAL!! NO WONDER SHE'S ONE OF KUREI'S MOST TRUSTED GUARDS!

WE WANT RECCA TO WIN, TOO.

IT'S OKAY...

CALM DOWN, MENO.

RECCA WON'T LOSE!!

BLINK

RIGHT NOW THOSE TWO ARE...

BUT...

WHAT'D YOU SAY ?!

RECCA !!

STAY OUT OF MY WAY, TOKIYA!

I'LL BEAT THEM BY MYSELF!!

DON'T ACT TOUGH.

GO TAKE A NAP.

I'M NOT SURE, BUT I THINK IT IS A...

ONE MISTAKE, AND HER MODAGU WILL TEAR YOU APART.

THIS IS NO TIME TO BICKER.

CORRECT, MISS NEON?

FUKYOWAON

BUT THAT KNOWLEDGE WON'T SAVE THEM.

IN FACT, I'LL SHOW YOU EXACTLY WHAT MY FUKYOWAON CAN DO. ♡

SWIK

KA-CHING. ♪

...

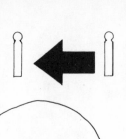

THERE ARE MANY VARIATIONS! THIS TALISMAN CONVERTS SOUND WAVES INTO ENERGY. IT SUCKS IN SOUND AND STORES IT LIKE A BATTERY!

THIS TALISMAN USES SOUND WAVES.

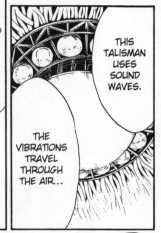

THE VIBRATIONS TRAVEL THROUGH THE AIR...

THEN THE FUKYOWAON DISCHARGES IT AS DESTRUCTIVE FORCE.

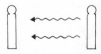

OH, LIKE A BLAST OF SOUND!

THAT'S WHAT MANGLED GENJURO...

I DIDN'T UNDERSTAND THAT.

LIKE FUJIN, IT CONTROLS WHAT THE EYES CAN'T SEE.

SAIHA

SO WHAT!!!

FWIP

102

THIS TALISMAN IS YAMABIKO, MOUNTAIN ECHO! IT REFLECTS SOUND WAVES!

SURPRISED?

HEE

HEE HEE

OW!!

SKRSH

CHANGED DIRECTIONS?!

THE SOUND...

THAT'S WHY I INSISTED ON A DOUBLE BOUT.

TOGETHER, WE ARE STRONGER THAN THE SUM OF OUR PARTS!!

EVEN IF I MISS, MIKI CAN REDIRECT THE BLAST!

DIRECT ATTACK

REBOUND ATTACK

SQUEEK

CIAO! ♡

WHOM

LET'S FINISH THEM OFF AND HAVE LUNCH!

WELL, YOU TWO WEREN'T MUCH.

TUMP!!

UNH...

WE TOOK THEM TOO LIGHTLY!!

STUPID TOKIYA CAN'T SEE HER EITHER?

WHAT AN INFERIOR, PATHETIC BROTHER...

IS HE REALLY MASTER KUREI'S BROTHER?

YOU'RE SUCH A FOOL.

YOU'RE JUDGING HIM BY THE INCIDENT AT THE MANSION.

AND I'M GONNA KILL HIM!!!

HMPH...

SHUT UP!! THAT GOON IS NOT MY BROTHER!!

YOU'LL NEVER BEAT MASTER KUREI.

AND GIRLS ARE NO EXCEPTION!!

HE WAS ONLY TOYING WITH YOU THAT TIME, LIKE TEASING A KITTEN WITH YARN...

YOUR DRAGON PROVIDED THE MIRACLE THAT SAVED YOU.

WHAT'D YOU SAY?

FIRST OF ALL...

FOUR OF THE 10 JUSSHIN-SHU ARE ON MASTER KUREI'S URUHA-KURENAI TEAM!!!

MASTER KUREI WAS USING LESS THAN 10 PERCENT OF HIS POWERS!!

AND SECOND...

URUHA-KURENAI IS...

FAR MORE LETHAL!!

THE OTHER URUHA TEAMS HAVE ONLY ONE JUSSHIN-SHU LIKE GENJURO OR ME.

YOU KNOW WHAT THIS MEANS DON'T YOU, KAORU? ♡

!

SHAKE

YOU'RE GOING TO DIE RIGHT NOW!

AND REASON THREE, AND THIS MAY BE THE BIGGEST REASON...

THIS IS FOR CALLING ME UGLY!!!

UNH...

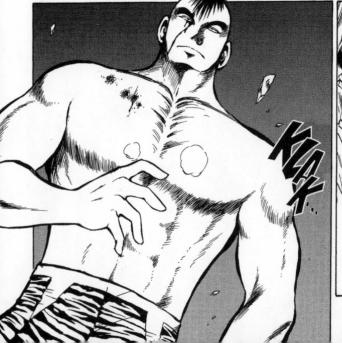

KLAK...

THE GIRLS DIDN'T KNOCK THEM OFF THE FLOOR!!

IT WAS--

115

I'VE HAD IT WITH YOU TWO ASSHOLES !!

GO HOME!

IF YOU DON'T WANT TO FIGHT...

I DON'T KNOW WHY YOU TWO ARE ACTING LIKE BRATS...

BUT YOU'RE PISSING ME OFF!

TOKIYA PROBABLY FEELS THE SAME!

FUKO AND I ALWAYS DREAMED OF KICKING YOUR ASS...

YOU KNOW, I NEVER LIKED YOU VERY MUCH, RECCA...

ER

K

THIS IS BIGGER THAN OUR PETTY DIFFER-ENCES!!

YANAGI IS ON THE LINE HERE! WE GOTTA WIN!!

BUT THAT'S THE PAST!!

WUP

WUP

I'M NOT GONNA LET YOUR STUPID PISSING CONTEST SCREW US UP!!!

AREN'T YOU A NINJA SWORN TO PROTECT HIS PRINCESS!!

WE GOTTA BE A TEAM.

THIS MAY SOUND CORNY, BUT...

119

SO, AS THE UMPIRE ...

I PENALIZE HOKAGE ONE POINT!!

YOU AIDED FIGHTERS WHO WERE ON THE FLOOR.

A NATURAL INSTINCT, BUT THERE'S A PENALTY!

SERVES HIM RIGHT, HA HA HA!!

DOMON NEGATED HIS OWN WIN!!

DOMON...

IF RECCA AND TOKIYA CAN WIN NOW...

THEN IT'S A SMALL PRICE TO PAY.

OKAY, FINE.

TMP

TMP

WHACK

LET THE FIGHT RESUME !!

YOU SHOULD HAVE PLAYED DEAD.

NOW YOU'RE GONNA DIE.

THEY'LL BE ALL RIGHT.

DON'T WORRY ...

THEY STILL LOOK MAD.

I WASTED MY BREATH ...

THEY'RE SUPPORTING EACH OTHER ...

THEY'LL BE ALL RIGHT.

THEY'RE FIGHTING IN DIFFERENT DIREC-TIONS.

MAYBE THEY'RE DOING IT UNCON-SCIOUSLY.

TOKIYA BACKED UP RECCA TWICE ALREADY TO WEAKEN THE BLOWS.

YANAGI SEES THINGS I CAN'T

I DIDN'T SEE THAT.

THANKS!!

I COULDN'T HAVE SAVED PRINCESS WITHOUT YOUR HELP!

RESHIN!

IT'S DIRTY AND SLIGHTLY USED, BUT IT'S ALL YOURS!

A HARD CREATURE TO UNDER-STAND!

SIMPLE-MINDED, STUPID, AND RECKLESS.

WHAT?

TMP

NEVER.

ARE YOU OUT OF BREATH?

SHWP

THOSE TWO ARE BEGINNING TO...

THEY'RE WORKING TOGETHER !!

I GET CAUGHT UP IN HIS PURPOSES ...

HE MAKES ME WANT TO BELIEVE ...

BUT STRANGELY ...

I HATE PEOPLE LIKE HIM.

SIMPLE-MINDED, STUPID, AND RECKLESS.

A HARD CREATURE TO UNDERSTAND.

RERK

WHAT WE WERE FIGHTING ABOUT!

TMP

I CAN'T REMEMBER ...

SO LET'S KICK SOME ASS !!!

Part Seventy-Five:
Live (7) Kurei, My Love

WHAT MADE THEM RECONCILE?!

HOW?

SISTER NEON...

PUSSIES, FEMINISTS, SISSIES...

THEY CALLED US COWARDS...

TOKIYA, WEREN'T THEY TALKING A LOT OF SHIT BEFORE THE FIGHT?

AND FINALLY CHICKENS...

READY FOR REVENGE

COULD THAT BE WHAT DID IT?!

WAS IT THAT ACROMEGALIC'S SPEECH?

GO, GO, TOKIYA! GO!

SWHP!

LET'S MAKE THEM EAT THOSE WORDS.

AND GET OUR PRIDE BACK!

WHAT'S WRONG, SAICHO?

THEY'RE BACK, FINALLY...

SHAKE

HE'S SCARY...

STOP TALKING BIG, HOKAGE!! JUST DIE ALREADY!!

GET 'EM GIRLS! RIP 'EM APART!!

RECCA MAY BE TOO TOUGH FOR ME NOW.

STRONGER THAN WHEN I FOUGHT HIM!!

SAICHO'S SASSING ME?

HAVEN'T YOU NOTICED? RECCA IS ...A

NO!!

ONCE YOU RECOVER...

WHAT, SAICHO? YOU FOUGHT WELL AGAINST HIM!

EVENTUALLY HE REALLY WILL BE ABLE TO USE ALL EIGHT DRAGONS AT ONCE!!

HE'S GETTING STRONGER IN EVERY FIGHT!

!!

BACK THEN, HE COULD CALL ON ONLY ONE DRAGON.

NOW HE CAN USE NADARE AND SAIHA AT THE SAME TIME!!

YOU DIDN'T KNOW?

WHAT'S WRONG?!

IT'S GONE!!

OR WAS THAT A FLUKE CAUSED BY HIS DESPERATION TO SAVE TOKIYA?

134

WHAT A SCARY KID ...

IF THERE'S EVEN GREATER POWER LURKING INSIDE HIM, HE MAY BECOME TOO STRONG FOR ME, TOO...

NO WAY.

INDEED ...

AS KUREI?

IS HE AS DEADLY ...

WHOOSH

WAP

!!

WHOOM

KOOF
...

MIKI!!

UGH...

THAT'S NOT HOW THE SAYING GOES.

HUH.

"IF THE BIRD SINGS FAST, SQUASH IT."

YOU BASTARDS!!

Y...

136

AND
...

AND MY SISTER AKI ...

FOR MY SISTER MIKI ...

MY SISTER SOLDIERS LOOK UP TO ME!

I ...

CAN'T LOSE!!

FOR MASTER KURE!!

KSSSH!!

A FIRE-RED ROSE.

IT WOULD LOOK LOVELY ON KURENAI.

YES...

HE SPOKE OF HIS MOTHER, WHO LIVED IN A FAR OFF LAND, AND OF A WOMAN NAMED KURENAI.

MASTER KUREI KEPT TO HIMSELF MOSTLY. BUT...

S F F

I WAS GLAD FOR KURENAI, AND WISHED THE TWO OF THEM HAPPINESS.

HIS FACE SOFTENED WHEN HE SPOKE OF KURENAI... I LIKED SEEING HIM LIKE THAT.

I WAS JUST A MAID, I COULDN'T BE JEALOUS. IT WASN'T MY PLACE.

NEON, THE JUSSHIN-SHU!

I AM ...

YOU'LL NEVER UNDERSTAND HIS GREATNESS!!

UNH ...

IT'S MY DUTY!!

BUT I WON'T LET YOU! I'LL STOP YOU HERE AND NOW!!

YOU LOSERS WANT TO HURT MASTER KURE!!

SWASH

PRELUDE!!

AS NEON OF THE FUKYO-WAON!!

AND NOW I CAN PROTECT MASTER KUREI!

HE EVADED IT EASILY!!

?!

WIP

KRAKK

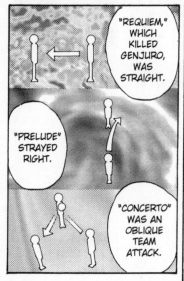

"REQUIEM," WHICH KILLED GENJURO, WAS STRAIGHT.

"PRELUDE" STRAYED RIGHT.

"CONCERTO" WAS AN OBLIQUE TEAM ATTACK.

I'VE MEMORIZED YOUR MOVES.

143

"FUGUE" WAS A CHUNK OF SOUND.

THAT'S ALL... ANY MISTAKES?

"SERENADE" WAS THREE STRAIGHT SOUNDS.

"RHAPSODY" WAS A POWER MOVE THAT CRACKED THE GROUND...

IS TOKIYA SMARTER THAN I THOUGHT?!

DID I UNDER-ESTIMATE THEM?

BA-BUMP

BA-BUMP

HE FIGURED IT OUT AFTER SEEING EACH ONLY ONCE?!

WUSP

SISTER NEON...

LET'S GIVE UP...

MASTER KUREI...

WE...

CAN'T WIN...

MASTER
KUREI!

HUH?

YOU STILL WANT TO FIGHT?!

YOU'RE FINISHED, GIVE UP!!

WHY AM I DOING THIS?!

I DON'T LIKE FIGHTING GIRLS.

YOU HOLD A GRUDGE WELL...

YOU'RE WEAK, RECCA. WE SHOULD CRUSH THEM.

Part Seventy-Six:

Live (8) Curtain Call

UNH...

DON'T DO IT!

NO! SISTER NEON!!

FORCE FIELD?

IT'S A...

VMM...

I'M SORRY...

PLEASE, RELEASE US!!

IF YOU HAVE TO DIE, LET US DIE WITH YOU!!

DON'T DO THIS!!

154

155

BUT IF WE DON'T KILL HER, WE'LL ALL DIE.

YOU FEEL SORRY FOR NEON, EH?

YOU THINK SHE'S LIKE YOU...

WHY ARE YOU HESITATING?

SHOO

I WON'T LET HER DO THAT.

TSURARA MAI-- ICICLE DANCE!

FUNERAL MARCH ...

DO IT ...

WHAT'RE YOU GONNA DO, TOKIYA?!

GOODBYE ...

MIKI, AKI...

TSURARA MAI: MOISTURE FROM ENSUI TRAVELS UNDERGROUND AND THRUSTS UP IN BLADES OF ICE. ONE MODE OF HYOMON-KEN.

WHAT?

THE LIGHT FROM MY THREE EYES FORMS AN IMPENETRA-BLE WALL.

I AM MADOKA ...THE FORCE FIELD IS MINE!!

A...

FORCE FIELD?

WIP

IT WORKED !!

WHAT A LONG SHOT...

YES !!

SWAK

OOF !!

BUT NOW I HAVE CHOSEN TO AID YOU MYSELF.

HMPH ...

YOU ARE A FOOL FOR SPARING AN ENEMY!!

I DID NOT KNOW WHY SAIHA, NADARE, AND HOMURA JOINED YOU.

WHY?

TMP

HOKAGE
VS.
URUHA-
OTO!!!

HOKAGE
IS THE
WINNER
!!

WRAAH

WHAT
?!

FUCK
...

...

YOU'RE
SOFT
ON
GIRLS,
RECCA.

YOU'RE
TOO
COLD-
BLOODED!!

GOOD
...

FIGHT!

BUT DIE
NEXT
TIME!!

WE OWE
YOU ONE,
HOKAGE!!

YEAH YAY HAH

168

DON'T BE ASHAMED!!

EVEN TOKIYA'S EARS ARE RED.

YOU ACT LIKE EISAKU YOSHIDA...

NYUK NYUK NYUK

WHAP WHAP

...

EISAKU YOSHIDA: FAMOUS JAPANESE ACTOR

HEE HEE!

BUT THEY WORRIED ME.

THE RIFT IS MENDED.

HOKAGE...

THEY SEEMED SO WARY OF EACH OTHER, BUT A BOND EXISTS BETWEEN THEM...

A BOND THAT CAN SURVIVE A FALLING OUT.

DON'T FORGET WHAT I'M ABOUT TO TELL YOU...

SHAAOO

THE ULTIMATE CHALLENGE AWAITS YOU IN THE SEMIFINALS!!

YOU'LL BOTH BE HISTORY SOON!!

YOU STILL HAVE TO FACE OTHER URUHA TEAMS!

NO MATTER HOW HARD YOU FIGHT, YOU GUYS WILL NEVER LEAVE HERE ALIVE!

WITH JISHO OF JISHOTO-- THE MAGNETIC SWORD!!

URUHA-KU-ROGANE! (IRON)

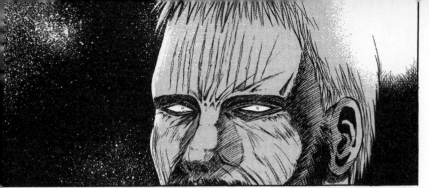

HE EVEN RIVALS KUREI.

HE'S PROBABLY THE DEAD-LIEST OF ALL URUHA.

YOU KNOW HIM, KAORU?

JISHO?

YES.

RECCA!

I'LL TAKE BACK CALLING YOU A PATHETIC...

BUT NOW YOU SHOULD GIVE UP AND DIE.

I GIVE YOU CREDIT FOR BEATING TWO URUHA TEAMS.

...

WHOA...

WOW! YOU'RE TOUGH!!

NEON ···

HUH?

NICE!

DON'T BE MAD.

WHO ARE YOU?!

SHUT UP!!

NO, REALLY!!

HE SAVED MY LIFE.

WAIT, RECCA.

NICE TO MEET YOU.

PEOPLE CALL ME "JOKER"...

MENO?

OH! THANKS, BUDDY!!

YAY...

WELL, I GOT TO SEE A GOOD FIGHT, ANYWAY.

I GOT SEPARATED FROM MY TEAM...LOOKS LIKE THEY'RE NOT HERE...

HIS FIGHTING AURA IS ABOUT AVERAGE.

YEAH... LIKE DAIKOKU OF KLI.

MAYBE HE ISN'T TOUGH.

YOU GUYS ARE HARSH!

...

YOU LOOK TOUGH.

WHICH TEAM?

TRUMP ...NO, I FORGOT WHAT WE'RE CALLED.

THEY TOOK ME, SO THEY'VE PROBABLY LOST BY NOW.

NAH...

LET'S TAKE A PEEK AT B BLOC!

HERE'S AN IDEA!

YOU GOTTA CHECK OUT THE OTHER BLOCS ONCE IN A WHILE!

WHAT DO YOU MEAN?!

I'LL ESCORT YOU PRETTY LADIES!

WE SHOULD CHECK OUT OUR POTENTIAL OPPONENTS...

WHAT DO YOU MEAN?!

OKAY!

PRETTY?

HMPH...

WANNA GO, RECCA?

HE'S FUNNY!

PFFT

174

NEXT UP: SHIN-SENGUMI VS. CIRCUS!!

I WANNA SEE THESE GUYS, BUT...

FINE.

I'LL GO...

BLOC B

URUHA-KUROGANE VS. URUHA-MA

JISHO?!

THAT'S...

!!

SHIT

WHAT ARE YOU DOING HERE?!

NEON?

WE MEET AGAIN...

← CHANGED CLOTHES

THEY USE THE MAGNETIC PULL OF NORTH AND SOUTH.

JISHO'S TWO SWORDS, THE JISHOTO, HAVE INFINITE FORM.

LOOKS LIKE YOU'LL BE FACING ...

THEY PICKED THE WRONG GUY TO FIGHT.

WHATEVER... IT'S URUHA VS. URUHA! THIS FIGHT IS THE BIG DRAW TODAY.

URUHA-MA IS FULL OF PEOPLE I DON'T KNOW...PROBABLY LOW-LEVEL TROOPS.

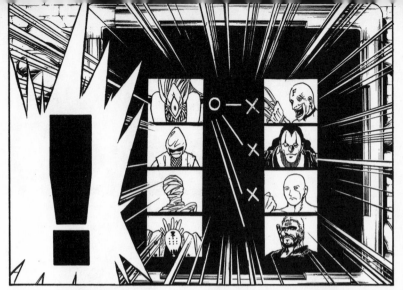

WHAT
!?!

WHA--

NEON
...

JISHO!!
WHAT'S
GOING
ON?!

WHAT
THE...ONE
FIGHTER IS
BEATING
JISHO'S
WHOLE
TEAM.

HOW
THE
HELL?

NEON
WAS
WRONG!

OOOOOO

BY THE WAY, GASHAKURA...

HOW MANY GUARDS DOES URUHA HAVE?

VERY WELL...

GRAAKR

THEY'RE CALLED JUSSHIN-SHU. THERE ARE 10 OF THEM.

OLDER BROTHER!

FOR BOTH OF US TO JOIN JUSSHIN-SHU, TWO MUST BE REMOVED.

SRUK

KLONK

IT'S HIS AMMUNI-TION.

THAT'S THE HEAD OF A URUHA-KUROGANE MAN...

THAT'S HOW HE FIGHTS.

WHAT! DIDN'T YOU SEE?

WHOA!! A HUMAN HEAD?!

MASTER KUREI SAID...

CH-CHAK

THE FITTEST RISE TO THE TOP, THAT'S NATURE'S WAY!

DAY THREE OF THE TOURNAMENT ENDED WITH EIGHT TEAMS REMAINING.

A BIG UPSET.

THIS IS...

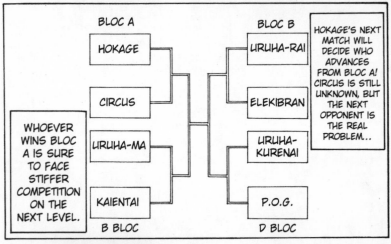

BLOC A

HOKAGE

CIRCUS

URUHA-MA

KAIENTAI

B BLOC

BLOC B

URUHA-RAI

ELEKIBRAN

URUHA-KURENAI

P.O.G.

D BLOC

HOKAGE'S NEXT MATCH WILL DECIDE WHO ADVANCES FROM BLOC A! CIRCUS IS STILL UNKNOWN, BUT THE NEXT OPPONENT IS THE REAL PROBLEM...

WHOEVER WINS BLOC A IS SURE TO FACE STIFFER COMPETITION ON THE NEXT LEVEL.

DON'T WORRY...

HUH?

T'UP

THEY'RE NOT IN MY SIGHTS.

...

To Be Continued!!

maison ikkoku™

fushigi yûgi™

GOLLANCZ MANGA

CASE CLOSED™

FLAME OF RECCA™

find out more at www.orionbooks.co.uk

fushigi yûgi ™

Welcome to the wonderfully exciting, funny, and heartfelt tale of Miaka Yûki, a normal high-school girl who is suddenly whisked away into a fictional version of ancient China.

fushigi yûgi
The Mysterious Play

fushigi yûgi
The Mysterious Play · VOL. 5: RIVAL

fushigi yûgi
The Mysterious Play
13: GODDESS

Charged with finding seven Celestial Warrior protectors, and given a mission to save her new world, Miaka encounters base villains and dashing heroes — and still manages to worry about where her next banquet is coming from.

FUSHIGI YUGI © Yuu WATASE/Shogakukan Inc.

find out more at www.orionbooks.co.uk

COMPLETE OUR SURVEY AND
LET US KNOW WHAT YOU THINK!

❑ Please do NOT send me information about Gollancz Manga, or other Orion titles, products, news and events, special offers or other information.

Name: _____

Address: _____

Town: _____ County: _____ Postcode: _____

❑ Male ❑ Female   Date of Birth (dd/mm/yyyy): __ / __ / _____
                    (under 13? Parental consent required)

What race/ethnicity do you consider yourself? (please check one)

❑ Asian   ❑ Black   ❑ Hispanic

❑ White/Caucasian   ❑ Other: _____

Which Gollancz Manga series did you purchase?

❑ Case Closed   ❑ Dragon Ball   ❑ Dragon Ball Z   ❑ Flame of Recca
❑ Fushigi Yûgi   ❑ Fushigi Yûgi: Genbu Kaiden   ❑ Maison Ikkoku
❑ One Piece   ❑ Rurouni Kenshin ❑ Yu-Gi-Oh!   ❑ Yu-Gi-Oh! Duelist

What other Gollancz Manga series have you tried?

❑ Case Closed   ❑ Dragon Ball   ❑ Dragon Ball Z   ❑ Flame of Recca
❑ Fushigi Yûgi   ❑ Fushigi Yûgi: Genbu Kaiden   ❑ Maison Ikkoku
❑ One Piece   ❑ Rurouni Kenshin ❑ Yu-Gi-Oh!   ❑ Yu-Gi-Oh! Duelist

How many anime and/or manga titles have you purchased in the last year?
How many were Gollancz Manga titles?

Anime	Manga	GM
❑ None	❑ None	❑ None
❑ 1-4	❑ 1-4	❑ 1-4
❑ 5-10	❑ 5-10	❑ 5-10
❑ 11+	❑ 11+	❑ 11+

Reason for purchase: (check all that apply)
- ❏ Special Offer
- ❏ Favourite title
- ❏ Gift
- ❏ In store promotion If so please indicate which store: _____
- ❏ Recommendation
- ❏ Other _____

Where did you make your purchase?
- ❏ Bookshop
- ❏ Comic Shop
- ❏ Music Store
- ❏ Newsagent
- ❏ Video Game Store
- ❏ Supermarket
- ❏ Other: _____
- ❏ Online: _____

What kind of manga would you like to read?
- ❏ Adventure
- ❏ Comic Strip
- ❏ Fantasy
- ❏ Fighting
- ❏ Horror
- ❏ Mystery
- ❏ Romance
- ❏ Science Fiction
- ❏ Sports
- ❏ Other: _____

Which do you prefer?
- ❏ Sound effects in English
- ❏ Sound effects in Japanese with English captions
- ❏ Sound effects in Japanese only with a glossary at the back

Want to find out more about Manga?
Look it up at www.orionbooks.co.uk, or www.viz.com

THANK YOU!
Please send the completed form to:

Manga Survey
Orion Books
Orion House
5 Upper St Martin's Lane
London, WC2H 9EA

All information provided will be used for internal purposes only.
We promise not to sell or otherwise divulge your details.

LD 3870642 3